JUNIOR

DATE DUE		
JUN.20.1996	DEC 07 '96	
JUL.11.1996	JUN 16'97	
	JUL 09 97	
AUG.07.1996	MAR 07'99	
SEP 0 5'96		
	MAY 11 '00	
	MAY 05 00	
SEP.19.1996	JUN 20 '00	
OCT 09'96	NOV 0 2 2004	
OCT 1 4 '96		
NOV 2 0 '96		

Jackson   5/96

County

Library

System

HEADQUARTERS:

413 W. Main

Medford, Oregon 97501

GAYLORD M2G

DARK DAY,
LIGHT NIGHT

DARK DAY,

LIGHT NIGHT

Jan Carr   Illustrated by James Ransome

Hyperion Books for Children
New York

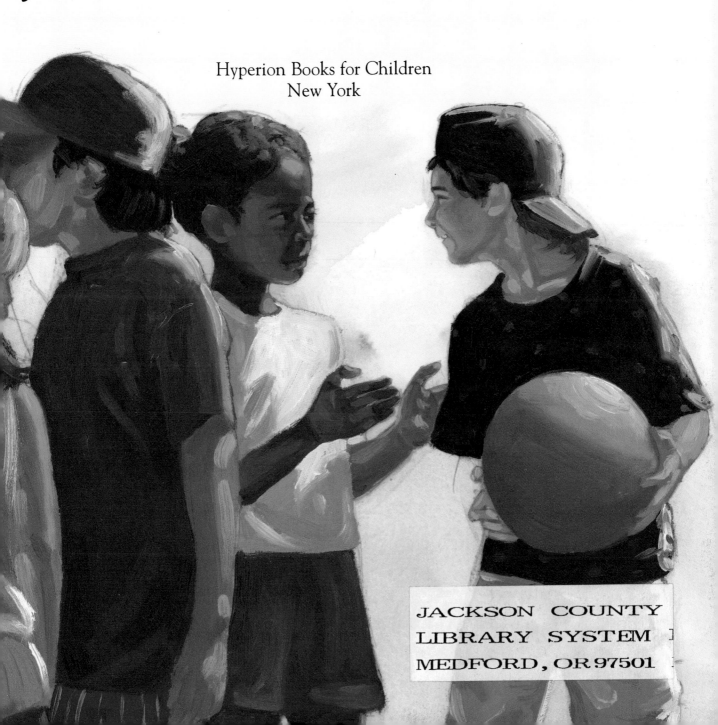

For Jessie, with love
—Aunt Jan

To my aunts Ruby, Minnie, Janet, Frances, Gloria, Jean,
and in special memory of my late Aunt Gladys
—James Ransome

Text © 1995 by Jan Carr.
Illustrations © 1995 by James Ransome.
All rights reserved.
Printed in Hong Kong by South China Printing Co. (1988) Ltd.
For information address Hyperion Books for Children,
114 Fifth Avenue, New York, New York 10011.
First Edition

1 3 5 7 9 10 8 6 4 2

Library of Congress Cataloging-in-Publication Data
Carr, Jan.
Dark day, light night/Jan Carr; illustrated by James Ransome—
1st ed.   p.   cm.
Summary: 'Manda's aunt Ruby helps her to deal with some angry
feelings by making lists of all the things that
they like in the world.
ISBN 0-7868-0018-6 (trade) — ISBN 0-7868-2014-4 (lib. bdg.)
[1. Aunts—Fiction.   2. Conduct of life—Fiction.]
I. Ransome, James, ill.   II. Title.
PZ7.C22947Dar   1994   [E]—dc20   93-45932   CIP   AC

Some days the whole world feels hateful, colorless like rain clouds, murky as mud. I wish Bobby would fall down flat. "And break both his legs!" I tell Aunt Ruby.

"Why don't you go out and get back in the game?" she asks.

"Because Bobby grabbed the ball right out of my hands!" I shout. I've told Aunt Ruby the whole story already. We've been through it at least ten times. "I'm getting under the covers," I say. "And *staying* there!"

Aunt Ruby peers at me through squint eyes. She tells me that when I get "this way" it might make me feel better if I can think of some things I like. She gets out a pencil and paper. "Go ahead, 'Manda," she says, "tell me what it is you like in this world."

Patches nudges me with his cold, wet nose.

"Nothing," I say.

Aunt Ruby writes that down. "Go on."

I can tell that she's not going to leave me alone until I come up with a better answer, so I say, "Beds," because that's the thing my eye's resting on. I say, "Pillows." I say, "Teddy bears, dresser drawers, big-old-wet dog snouts." I rattle off everything I see in the room. I figure that should do it.

Aunt Ruby thinks otherwise. "Wider," she says.

I think of Bobby and how he laughed at me when he grabbed the ball away. "So what's so great about liking anything?" I ask.

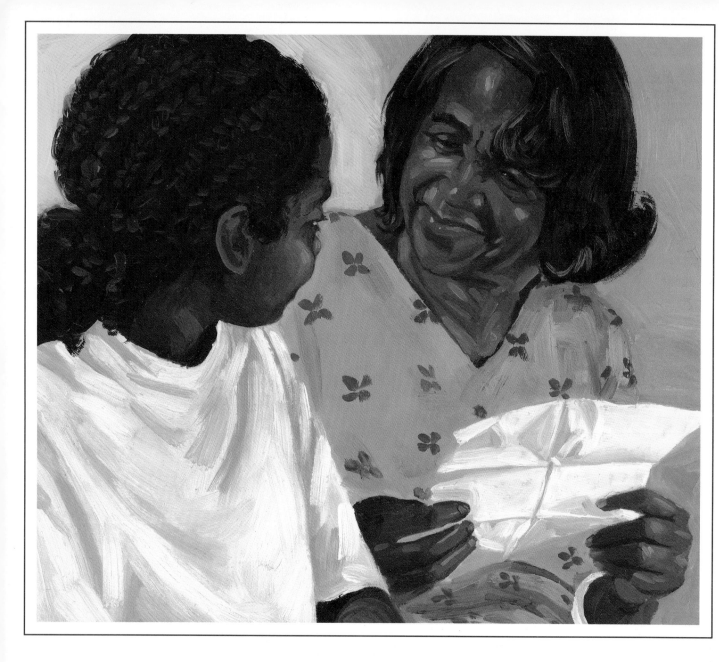

Aunt Ruby's lips twitch into a smile. She looks out the
window. "The light fades late this time of year," she says, as if
that's some kind of answer.

Then Aunt Ruby pulls another piece of paper from her
pocket. This one's all folded up and worn thin at the creases. "I
have a list of my own," she says.

"You do? How come?"

"Because." She winks. "Sometimes I feel like you do now."

Aunt Ruby invites me into the crook of her arm, and I nestle there while she reads her list out loud. Aunt Ruby has a voice deep as dusk and hushed as trees. I close my eyes so I can see everything she describes.

"One thing I like," she says, "is that cream-colored tom that visits our window. I like to set out a bowl of food for him and watch the pretty way he licks his paws after he finishes his dinner and his belly's happy and full."

"Meow," I say. I bare my claws and scratch at the air.

Aunt Ruby reads on. "On hot nights like these I like it when your mama takes down the big china bowl and mixes together blueberries and strawberries, chunks of peaches and any other sweet, bright fruit we bought that day at market."

"All the colors together are like painting a picture," I say.

"Aren't they? All the juices glistening . . ."

"Music," I pipe in. "Is music on the list?"

"It is indeed. I like it when old Mr. Franklin comes over to play his saxophone and Callie drifts in along with the heat and gets to singing along."

"She sings sweet."

"Sweet as sunshine."

"Sunshine!" I cry out. "Did you write sunshine down?"

"Right here. But some days," Aunt Ruby continues, dark suddenly, hinting danger, "I like it when a storm blows in. When the sky sparks up lightning and the wind makes a mess of things just because it feels like it."

"You do?"

"Well, sure." She chucks my chin. "As long as you and I are safe inside.

"And when winter comes I like to bundle us up in woolly layers so when we go outside we're cozy warm."

"You and me and Patches," I say. I run my fingers through Patches's sleek, warm coat. I whistle high, like winter wind.

"What else?" I change the subject. I snuggle deeper into Aunt
Ruby's arm.

"Well, when there's something special to celebrate I like to put
on a flouncy dress and pin doodads in my hair and paint up my
face like a queen."

"Me, too!" I shout.

"Oh, and I like the tight, damp curls on babies' heads. You had tight little curls, you know that?"

"I did?"

"Tight-tight. Like they'd been pinned up in the womb."

I look out the window at my friends playing. Aunt Ruby joins me. She shakes her head, just looking. "What a pretty mess of children out there. All the many-shaded skins we're born to. All the beautiful faces."

"Look," I notice. "The moon's out."

"So it is. Fat and full." Aunt Ruby makes a sound that might be a sigh, but it sounds more like a purr—creamy, like our tom.

She starts to fold up her list. "And don't think I forgot the most important thing of all," she says. She plants a kiss on my forehead. "I like *you*."

"You do?" I whisper. I feel a little shy. Aunt Ruby's got me thinking that I like me pretty much, too.

Outside my window Bobby's caught the ball. He's holding it high above his head, like some kind of big shot, but I know better. *I like to play ball,* I think. *And sometimes, when he's nice, I even like to play with Bobby.* Aunt Ruby guesses at the thoughts buzzing in my brain.

"You know," she says, "you still have time to go out and play a while before it's time for bed."